Class Six and the Very Big Rabbit

Written by Martin Waddell
Illustrated by Tony Ross

Collins

1 Rabbits are nice

Class Six liked their teacher, Miss Bennett. She could do magic, like no one else could. She could wiggle her ears and make things disappear. Then she'd earwiggle again, and make them come back.

One day she did something different. She was reading Class Six a book about rabbits.

"Rabbits *are* nice," Miss Bennett said. Then she grinned and earwiggled. "I wish I was a rabbit!" she said.

And ... there was a fizzzz...
and a flash ...
and a bang...

... and Miss Bennett changed into a very big rabbit.

4

Class Six sat and looked at the very big rabbit,
and the very big rabbit sat looking right back
at Class Six.

She was Miss Bennett-sized, and she had glasses like Miss Bennett. She was holding the book Miss Bennett had been reading, so Class Six knew it had to be her. They just didn't know how she had managed the trick.

Everyone cheered the big rabbit.

The big rabbit went back to the rabbit book and started reading again. At least she tried to read, but all that came out were squeaks.

"Rabbits can't read," Ranjit whispered to Rachel.

"You can't blame her for trying," Rachel whispered back.

2 Something's gone wrong!

"It's a cool trick, Miss Bennett," Ranjit told
the big rabbit politely. "The best trick that I've
ever seen, but we think it's time you went back
to being Miss Bennett."

The big rabbit earwiggled again, and she squeaked.

"Something's gone wrong with the wishing!" Ranjit whispered to Rachel.

"I don't think she knows what to do," Rachel said.

The big rabbit froze.

"That's what rabbits do when they're caught, and can't think of a way to escape," Ranjit told Rachel. "Miss Bennett's got stuck as a rabbit and doesn't know how to wish herself back."

"We'll have to tell the Head," Rachel decided.

"The Head will be cross with Miss Bennett,"
Ranjit pointed out.

The big rabbit rubbed her nose with her big paw.

"Okay," Ranjit said. "Someone fetch the Head!"

Class Six looked worried. No one wanted to go to
the Head.

"We'll be told off for telling silly stories!"
said Rachel.

"You'll just have to tell her yourself," Ranjit told
the big rabbit. "When she sees you're so huge,
she'll know that you're not just an ordinary rabbit."

12

The big rabbit made for the door.

"Stop!" Rachel called, and she pulled the big rabbit back. "If the little ones see a huge rabbit coming, they'll be scared out of their wits."

Rachel was right, as usual, and she worked out what to do about it.

"We'll dress up our big rabbit so she looks like Miss Bennett!" Rachel told the whole class.

And that's what Class Six did.

3 This rabbit is ME!

Miss Bennett's coat was in her cupboard.
Rachel put it on the big rabbit.

The big rabbit's paws couldn't manage
the buttons. Rachel did up the buttons for her.

Ranjit squeezed Miss Bennett's gloves on to her front paws.

Rachel put Miss Bennett's hat on her head.

"You look lovely!" Rachel told the big rabbit. "*Almost* as nice as Miss Bennett."

The big rabbit looked very pleased.

"It looks like a big rabbit disguised as Miss Bennett to me," said Ranjit.

They walked through the school with the rabbit disguised as Miss Bennett. The big rabbit walked in the middle, with Class Six all around her, so no one could see her big rabbit feet.

They knocked on the Head's door.

"Who's there?" called the Head.

"Class Six and a very big rabbit," Ranjit replied.

The Head opened the door.

"Please, Miss," Rachel said. "Our Miss Bennett turned herself into a big rabbit."

"Gosh!" said the Head. "I've never seen a rabbit that big. Are you *sure* that this rabbit is really Miss Bennett?"

The big rabbit pulled her gloves off with her big rabbit teeth. Then she picked up the writing pad and a pencil from the Head's desk.

She wrote: *This rabbit is ME!* And she signed the note: *Dorothy Bennett*.

"You've been earwiggling again, Dorothy!"
the Head scolded. "Wish yourself back at once,
and stop being a rabbit!"

The big rabbit shrugged.

4 How can we help?

"Please, Miss," Rachel said. "We don't think Miss Bennett *can* wish herself back because she can't talk, only squeak."

And the big rabbit nodded her head.

"Oh dear, you've done it this time, Dorothy," the Head told the rabbit. "Looks like you'll have to stay a big rabbit for ever."

"How can we help?" Rachel said, trying to think.

"We could fetch her some lettuce and carrots," Ranjit suggested.

The big rabbit turned up her nose.

"Wait!" Rachel said. "Suppose *we* did the wishing for Miss Bennett?"

"Well, it *might* work," said the Head.

The big rabbit looked hopeful.

"We'll all wish together," said Rachel.
"And the big rabbit must wiggle her ears
while we're doing our wishing!"

The big rabbit clapped her paws together and
squeaked, as if to say **YES**!

"ONE-TWO-THREE!" said the Head.

And everyone shouted, "WE WISH OUR
MISS BENNETT WAS BACK!" while the big rabbit
wiggled her ears.

There was a fizzzz ...
and a flash ...
and a bang ...

... and the big rabbit was gone, and there was
Miss Bennett.

"Wow! What a relief!" gasped Miss Bennett.

"You can say that again," muttered the Head.

Then Miss Bennett thanked everyone in Class Six for their wishing, especially Ranjit and Rachel.

"That's the last time we'll see our big rabbit!" sighed Rachel.

But Ranjit found a new book on the Class Six reading shelf. It was about crocodiles.

Ranjit gave it to Miss Bennett ...

... and hoped.

Address: @ www.warren_school.com

TEACHER TURNS INT

By Class Six Repor

Something very exciting happened in Class Six this week. The teacher, Miss Bennett, wiggled her ears and said, "I wish I was a rabbit!" – and with a fizz, a flash and a bang, she turned into a very big !

In 's words: "There was an enormous FLASH, vanished and a big appeared in her place. It was like magic!"

"We knew the big was because she was reading her , " said .

But the very big turned out to have a very big problem. She couldn't turn back into .

BIG, FURRY RABBIT!

Ranjit and Rachel

It was time for Class Six to take action!

They disguised the big in Miss Bennett's

coat, hat and gloves and took her to see .

"We didn't want to scare the little ones,"

said .

Then and all  shouted together,

"WE WISH OUR WAS BACK!" while

the big wiggled her ears. Once again,

there was a fizz, a flash and a bang and

the big turned back into .

 said "Thank you, Class Six. I promise to be

more careful with my earwiggling."

✿ Ideas for guided reading ✿

Learning objectives: understand how dialogue is presented in stories and how paragraphing is used to organise dialogue; be aware of the different voices in stories using dramatised readings, showing difference between narrator and different characters; use talk to organise roles and action.

Curriculum links: Citizenship; Taking Part; Choices.

Interest words: disappear, earwiggle, fizzzz, flash, squeaks, whispered, politely, worried, ordinary, squeezed, disguised, relief, sighed, crocodile

Word count: 918

Getting started

This book can be read over two guided reading sessions.

- Ask the children to look at the back cover and discuss the text. Discuss what the story is about and ask children to predict what might happen in the story. *What could it be that went so very wrong?*

- Ask the children to skim through pp2–7 and establish who the main characters are (Miss Bennett, Ranjit and Rachel). Discuss what the different characters' voices might be like, and model their voices.

- Now read (pp2–7), checking the children are using the modelled voices and reading with expression. Discuss how punctuation and bold and italic print affect expression, and point out the use of paragraphs to indicate when different characters are speaking.

Reading and responding

- Ask the children to recap Class Six's problem on p7. How can they help Miss Bennett change back to normal? Ask them to read on quietly and independently up to p29.

- Ask them to look out for interesting or unfamiliar words in the text such as *'whispered' 'politely'* and note these down in their word books.

- Ask the children to list words that they can think of which will describe the different characters (e.g. *friendly, polite, magical,* etc).